# The Bremen Town Musicians

# The Bremen Town Musicians

## retold and illustrated by HANS WILHELM

SCHOLASTIC INC.
New York  Toronto  London  Auckland  Sydney

*To Maurice Sendak*

ISBN 0-590-44796-3

Copyright © 1992 by Hans Wilhelm, Inc.
All rights reserved. Published by Scholastic Inc.

12 11 10 9 8 7 6 5 4 3 2          9          3 4 5 6 7/9

Printed in the U.S.A.                    08

Designed by Adrienne M. Syphrett

The illustrations in this book were done in ink and watercolor.

**T**here was once a donkey
whose master made him carry sacks
to the mill year after year.
Now the donkey was getting old,
and his strength began to fail.

When the master realized that the donkey
was of no use to him anymore,
he decided to get rid of him.
But the donkey guessed
that something bad was in the wind,
so he made up his mind to run away.

He thought he would take the road to Bremen,
where he might get an engagement as a town musician.

On the way,
he found a dog lying by the side of the road,
panting as if he had been running for a long time.
"Now, Holdfast, why are you so out of breath?"
asked the donkey.

"Oh, dear!" said the dog. "I am old and getting weaker
every day, and I can no longer hunt.
My master was going to kill me, but I escaped!
Now how am I to make a living?"

"I will tell you what," said the donkey.
"I am going to Bremen to become a town musician.
Come with me. I can play the lute,
and you can beat the drum."

The dog liked the idea, and they walked on together.

It was not long before they came to a cat sitting by
the roadside, looking as dismal as three wet days.
"Now then, what is the matter with you, old Whiskerwiper?"
asked the donkey.

"Who can be cheerful when his life is in danger?"
answered the cat. "Now that I am old, my teeth are getting blunt,
and I'd rather sit by the fire than chase after mice.
Because of this, my mistress wanted to drown me,
so I ran away. But now I don't know what is
to become of me."

"Come with us to Bremen," said the donkey,
"and be a town musician. You know how to serenade."

The cat liked the idea and went along with them.

Soon the three runaways passed by a yard.
A rooster was perched on top of the gate,
crowing as loudly as he could.
"Your cries are breaking my heart," said the donkey.
"What is the matter?"

"Tomorrow is Sunday, and I have foretold good weather,"
said the rooster, "but my mistress is expecting guests
and has ordered the cook to cut off my head
and put me in the soup.
Therefore, I cry with all my might
while I still can."

"You'd better come along with us, Redhead," the donkey said.
"We are going to Bremen to become town musicians.
We could do with a powerful voice like yours."

This sounded perfect to the rooster, so all four went on together.

But Bremen was too far to be reached in one day.
Towards evening they came to a forest
where they decided to spend the night.

The donkey and the dog lay down under a huge tree,
the cat found a place among the branches,
and the rooster flew up to the top of the tree where he felt safe.
But before he went to sleep, the rooster looked all around
to the four points of the compass.
Suddenly he saw a small light shining in the distance.

He called out to his friends,
"There must be a house over there."

"Let's go and see," said the donkey,
"for this place is not very comfortable."

"And there might be
a few bones," said the dog.

They all set off in the direction of the light.
It grew larger and larger until it led them
to a robber's house, all lighted up.

The donkey — who was the tallest —
went to the window and looked in.
"Well, what do you see?" asked the dog.

"What do I see?" answered the donkey.
"I see a table loaded with wonderful
things to eat and to drink. And
robbers are sitting around the table,
having a great time!"

"That would be perfect for us!"
said the rooster.

"Yes, indeed," replied the donkey.
"I wish we were there."

The four friends put their heads together
to decide how they might scare off the robbers.
Finally they knew what to do.

The donkey placed his forefeet on the windowsill.
The dog got on the donkey's back,
the cat stood on the top of the dog, and lastly,
the rooster flew up and perched
on the cat's head.

At a given signal, they all
began to perform their music.
The donkey brayed,
the dog barked,
the cat meowed,
and the rooster crowed!

Then they burst into the room,
breaking the windowpanes.
The robbers fled at the dreadful noise.
They thought it was some goblin
and ran to the forest in the utmost terror.

The four friends sat down at the table
and feasted as if they hadn't eaten for weeks.
When they had finished they put out the lights
and looked for places to sleep.
The donkey found a comfortable spot outside,
the dog lay down behind the door,
the cat curled up on the hearth by the warm ashes,
and the rooster settled himself in the loft.
And since they were all very tired from their long journey,
they soon fell asleep.

In the forest, from a safe distance away,
the robbers were watching the house the whole time.
Shortly after midnight they saw that no light was burning
and that everything appeared peaceful.

"We shouldn't have been such cowards and run away!"
said their leader, and he ordered one of them
to go back and check out the house.

The robber went into the house and found everything very quiet.

He went into the kitchen to strike a light, and the cat woke up.
Thinking that the cat's glowing eyes were burning coals,
the robber held a match to them in order to light it.
The cat did not find this funny. He flew into the robber's
face, spitting and scratching.

The robber screamed in terror
and ran to get out through
the back door. But the dog,
who was lying there, leaped up
and bit the robber's leg.

The frightened robber rushed into
the yard where the donkey
struck out and gave him
a great kick with his hind foot.

And the rooster,
who had been wakened
by the noise, cried his loudest
"Kee-ka-ree-kee!"

The robber ran back to the others
as fast as he could,
and said, "Oh, dear!
In that house there is a gruesome witch.
I felt her breath, and she scratched me
with her long nails.
And by the door there stands a monster
who stabbed me in the leg with a knife.
And in the yard there lies a fierce giant
who beat me with a club.
And on the roof
there sits a judge
who cried, 'Bring the thief to me!'
I got out of that place as fast as I could!"

This scared the robbers so much that they never
went back to that house again.

And the four musicians liked their new home
so much that they stayed forever
and never went to Bremen Town at all.

## A Note from the Author

"Having been born and raised in Bremen, I have always had a special fascination for this old story of the donkey, the dog, the cat, and the rooster," says Hans Wilhelm, author/artist of more than 100 books for children.

"Like all Grimm fairy tales the story speaks on many levels. First, there is the obvious plot, which is touching, funny, exciting, and has a happy ending — at least for the animals!

"And then there are those mysterious elements that suggest a much deeper meaning: Why these particular animals? Why do they meet on a Saturday? Who are the robbers?

"I was so intrigued by this last question that I thought it would be interesting to identify the robbers in my version. But because I felt it was imperative to keep the text as close to the original German as possible, the identification comes only in the illustrations. (Have you noticed that the four robbers bear a striking resemblance to the ex-owners of the 'musicians'?)

"I have heard and read this story since early childhood, and with this new version, I hope to make the tale as much fun for children today as it has always been for me."